For Jonathan and Rowan Stubbs, with love

First US edition 2021

Library of Congress Catalog Card Number pending
ISBN 978-1-5362-1271-6

20 21 22 23 24 25 TLF 10 9 8 7 6 5 4 3 2 1

Printed in Dongguan, Guangdong, China

This book was typeset in WB Rachel Stubbs.
The illustrations were done in ink and graphite and finished digitally.

Candlewick Press
99 Dover Street
Somerville, Massachusetts 02144

www.candlewick.com

CANDLEWICK PRESS

MY RED HAT

Rachel Stubbs

I give you my hat.

It will keep you warm and dry

or help keep you cool.

It can be used for silly things,

serious things,

or necessary things.

It will help you stand out
in a crowd . . .

or not.

This hat holds dreams,

hides secrets,

and covers fears.

It is full of possibility.

With it you can go anywhere:

way down deep

or way up high . . .

wherever your feet may carry you . . .

until home calls you back

to where you belong.

This hat is for you.